Underneath it All

"My Story Is Your Story"

CiCi Smallz

Acknowledgments

Giving honor to God, who is the head of my life, I truly thank Him for continuing to watch over me, my son, and family. He continues to make a way when there seems to be no way. I give Him all praises for continuing to be my strength in the time of trouble. I don't know where I would be without Him in my life. He continues to keep me even in times when I didn't want to be here anymore. With him by my side my life began to change. I thank the Lord for helping me complete this greatest accomplishment. I want to inspire other young people. This was a hard journey but I still managed to not give up. God was there with me until my finished project was officially DONE!!!!!!

I want to thank K.D. Harris for believing in me and my work. You never gave up on me even when I was giving you a hard time. I truly appreciate you helping me accomplish such an amazing thing in my life. If it wasn't for you then my book would've never came to past. "The Purposed Pen Project" helped me to get started and taught me how to write my books. You're a great coach!!!! Thanks a lot K.D., love you girlie!!

I want to give a special thanks to my "UNC" Noah P. Jones for being there for me just in the nick of time. Without your readiness, patience and expertise, finishing this book would have been impossible. I'm forever grateful for you!

Shout out to my handsome baby boy that changed my whole life, my little Prophet Damarion Lyonelle George Smallwood. Mommy loves you so much son. Thank you for changing my world. I'm so glad that God blessed me with you. When I'm down, you make me happy. When I'm sad you find a way to make me smile. When I don't want to be bothered, you always find a way to make me laugh. I love you so much from the bottom of my heart. You are an angel that was sent into my life. We had a lot of ups and downs. We took many blows. Writing this book was a dream come true. I'll always have something to cherish along with you.

Special thanks to my mother, Stacy M. Evans, for everything you did. Thank you for assuring me that I would be successful in life; for teaching me to not worry about what people say, for teaching me to focus on my dreams, and for always being there for me. I know that I put you through hell throughout my life, but I thank God for you and all of your support. You were there through the things I had to grow up around and deal with. Even in that turmoil, you continued to smile and love me deeply. Mom, you are an angel in my eye and I don't know what I would do without you. I am the split image of you and you raised me to be an amazing young lady with a great future. I just want to tell you that I love you so much from the bottom of my heart.

Special thanks to my father, Darrell Smallwood Sr., for always letting me know how intelligent and wise of a young lady I was growing up. I could always count on you. I thank you for not letting me down when I was playing high school ball. You continued to push me and help me until I drew a foul, LOL. I love you from the bottom of my heart, you are a great father, and I thank God for allowing you to be my dad.

Thank you so much to my wonderful grandmother, Viola. I'm so glad you are in my life, we act so much alike. You are funny, loving, super sweet and have a big heart just like me I thank God for an amazing person like you. I love you to pieces Mom-Mom.

Thank you to my brothers and sisters: Joseph, Darielle, Darrell, Tiara, Travis and Blessed. I appreciate all of you for loving me. Even though y'all joke all the time I know that you guys believe in me and truly understand my calling. So I love y'all and thanks for pushing me forward in my journey with God. I'm so glad to be your sister and just want to say that I am so happy that you guys are supporting me every step of the way.

I also want to send special thanks to my aunts and uncles: Janice Robinson (continue to rest in God), George Lynch Jr. (continue to rest in God), Jethreo and Cheryl Tickles, Gladys Triplett, Peachie Wright (continue to rest in God), Muhammad and Vicki Mustafa, Theresa Lynch, and Raymond Jackson. I appreciate everything that all of you did for me. Thanks for taking me under all of your wings when I needed you. I love all of you for that and I thank God for sending all of you into my life. You guys continue to let me know how my life is changing with God and I appreciate y'all.

Thank you to all of my nieces and nephews for allowing me to be your super aunt. LOL! I appreciate the love that you all continue to show.

All of you put a smile on my face every time I see you and that truly blesses me. Thanks for everything you do and say. From all of the good conversations and wonderful laughs we share with all the hugs and kisses. Joseph III, Jasmine, Jahzara, Jordyn, Da'Jhane, and Zakari. I will forever be your super auntie. I love you from the bottom of my heart.

Thank you to all of my cousins who helped out with anything I needed concerning me and my son. I really appreciate all of your love and support. All of you continue to push me to go on in God and constantly ask that I pray for you. I love you all and want you to know that I'm truly grateful to have cousins like you.

Also, to my extended siblings: Myesha, Alonzo, Tae, Damiah, Boo Boo and Dai-Dai. I appreciate y'all for taking me in as a sister and loving me. You guys are something special in my heart and I truly thank God for all of you being a part of my life. All of you are like my best friends. It makes me feel good to hear y'all address me as "HEY SIS" every time I see you. Thanks for all of your encouragement and support throughout my life. Thanks for sharing your Mom & Dad with me LOL!!!!

Also to my extended nieces Milan, Theory, Auliya and Qorah. I appreciate all of you for allowing me to be your aunt. All of the laughs and fun times we share is truly a blessing. I am so glad I got to meet wonderful beauties like you. Auntie CiCi loves all of you.

Special thanks to my awesome, amazing, biggest supporters and motivators. My wonderful Pastors: Senior Pastor LaShele Jones-Evans, and Deacon Damion Evans Sr. I appreciate the both of you so much for continuing to be my shoulder when I needed to cry and someone to talk to. You guys always help me to grow in God in so many ways. You never let me fail, even when I would say I hate living this church life. Y'all are my mentors, second parents and life coaches. I don't know where I would be if God haven't sent the both of you in my life. Both of you helped me get through some tough times in my life. You teach me to draw strength from God when I needed it. You taught me how to build up a prayer life, read the Word of God and fast to get the enemy off my back. Pastor LaShele you taught me how to be a strong mother and take care of your godson. Deacon Damion you help me to understand that sometimes things happen in life for a reason. You will always be there to set the example for your godson no matter what. Thanks for taking me in as y'all daughter and even allowing me to spend time with y'all as a family. The both of you keep me smiling and I know that I can count on you. Every hug counts and every talk helped to get me to the place where I am today. Thank You So Much! Love Y'all From The Bottom Of My Heart!

Thank you very much to my Special Nana Apostle Linda Henry for everything you did to push me to the next level. I truly love you from the bottom of my heart and appreciate every prayer and encouraging word you spoke into my life.

Thanks to Pastor Subina Blanding. You have been an inspiration to my spiritual walk. Your constant encouragement and prayers have helped me stay focused and not give up. Your push keeps me praying and in the Word. You have been a true blessing in my life. I love you so much from the bottom of my heart.

Thanks to my lovely extended aunts and uncles, Minister Leslie Jones, Minister Keisha McKenzie, Tiffany Jones, Pastor Jordan and Lady Keona Robinson, Minister Je'Nae Henderson, Pastor Antoine and Lady Michelle Brumble,

Apostle AJ and Pastor Taneya Harding, Pastor Tilaki Barksdale-Britt, Elizabeth Ceaser, Pastor Jamila Monroe, Pastor Dayna DeVine, Apostle Leonette Davis-Collins, Pastors David and Cheryl Brown, Pam Murray, Apostle Tameka Stanford-Daniels, Pastor David and Prophetess Jocelyn Fitzgerald, Apostle Teresa Hicks, Pastor Ronnell and Elder Kimberly Waples, Anita Woody, Larry Woody Sr.(continue to rest in God), Pierre and Tina Lofland. You all are such a tremendous blessing and play a major part in my life. I truly admire you all and appreciate that God allowed you to be in my life. Thank you very much for all that you do for me. The words of wisdom, encouragement, and motivation help me. I love all of you from the bottom of my heart. Thank you for believing in me and letting me know that there is greatness inside of me.

To my wonderful, amazing, and loving Godparents, Melvin and Darlene Dillard, Apostle Jeffery and Prophetess Lisa Carter, Apostle Crystal DeWar, Mamie Simmons, Ministers Terence and Artisha Hall, Rhonda Williams (continue to rest in God) and Kissa Smith. Thank you all for caring for me and loving me like your own. I appreciate all of you and thank God for allowing you to lead and guide me in the right direction. You continue to push me and see that I carry a great anointing on my life. You never stopped praying for me and I truly appreciate that God sent all of you into my life for a great cause. Being your Goddaughter is truly a blessing.

I love all of my God sisters and God brothers. I'm so happy that you guys never gave up on me. Thank you so much for having my back and pushing me forward so I could reach my destiny.

Special thanks to my wonderful big sis, Elder Alicia Blanding, who is always there when I need her. You're an amazing supporter and will forever have my back. I appreciate you so much girlie. You are my mentor and you never let me fail. You are the strength that keeps me going in God. Thanks love you to the fullest BIG SIS!!!!!!

Also want to say thank you to Debbie, Mar, Moni, Mia, Kee Kee,Quizzy, and Mir for always being there when I needed you, treating me with love and kindness, always lending a helping hand with my little boy. Thanks, all of you are the best. I love all of you from the bottom of my heart.

To the Howard Wildcat Family thank you all for inspiring me to keep my head up and maintain my focus on becoming a Class of 2013 Howard graduate. I love all of you, Coach Curtis Clack, Tena V. Gladney, Lori Thompson-Hayes, and Ronda Laws. Every day that I got in trouble y'all would always want to talk to me so that I wouldn't get kicked out of school. All of you believed I had a bright future ahead of me. The moment you guys saw me walk across the stage at The Bob Carpenter Center y'all were well pleased and I appreciate that you never gave up on me. Thank you for all that you did for me and your support that helped me become the young woman that I am today.

Thanks a lot Ms. Emily. You were pushing me to complete school as a Medical Assistant at Dawn Career Institute. You were an amazing teacher and great motivator to help me reach my goal. Even when I wanted to give up you know that I could do it and maintain good grades even with everything that I was going through as a young mother. You didn't stop being on me until I finally walked across that stage at The Chase Center with a 4.0 GPA. Thanks Girlie Love You!!!!!

Thank you to my two best friends, Derricka Washington-Crosby and Mahogany Gamble. I appreciate you both being there for me when I needed you. I love you both so much.

Most of all, a big shout out to my wonderful church family. Thank you for continuing to pray for me. Thank you for your help through the process of overcoming obstacles and reaching my destiny. I appreciate it so much; I don't know where I would be without you and God. Heaven Touched Outreach Ministries, you rock! Let's keep striving for greatness.

To all those who picked up this book, Thank you for supporting my dream. This is just the beginning. Stop by my Facebook page and tell me what you think.

www.facebook.com/GreatestKreation

Thank you! I love you all so much!

God Bless!!!!!!

Dedication

Pastor George W. & Evangelist Emily R. Lynch

Rest In Paradise

I want to dedicate this book to these two amazing people, my guardian angels: Mom-Mom & Pop-Pop. I love and miss y'all very much. Keep smiling down on me and watching over me. I know you're in a better place now. Thanks for all y'all did for me from a child to a teenager. I will never forget y'all. I'm so glad that God made me your granddaughter. Continue to rest in God. Y'all will forever me in my heart your gone but not forgotten love you

Liberty of Congress Control Number: In publication data

ISBN: 978-0-9991590-5-7

Underneath it All

"My Story Is Your Story"

Author: CiCi Smallz

Interior Design: Ciara K. Smallwood & LaShele Jones-Evans

Cover Design: LaShele Jones-Evans & www.fiverr.com/Amjed_viera

Editor: Noah P. Jones

Published By: Ciara K. Smallwood

This is a work of fiction. It is not meant to depict, portray or represent any particular real person. All the characters, incidents, and dialogues are the products of the author's imagination and are not to be construed as real. Any references or similarities to actual events, entities, real people, living or dead, or to real locales are intended to give the novel a sense of reality. Any similarity in other names, characters, entities, places, and incidents is entirely coincidental. All rights reserved, including the right of reproduction in whole or part in any form.

Table of Contents

Introduction

Psalm 34:17-20 "When the righteous cry for help, the Lord hears and delivers them out of all their troubles. The Lord is near to the brokenhearted and saves the crushed in spirit. Many are the afflictions of the righteous, but the Lord delivers him out of them all. He keeps all his bones; not one of them is broken."

Princess really didn't understand the true meaning of that scripture until she experienced it herself. Life dealt her a hand of abandonment, rejection, bullies, molestation, depression, and feeling like an unfit parent. This story is taking you through Princess' journey from her childhood to adulthood. She was lost without any hope. As a young girl, Princess deals with so much hurt and pain. She hid it so well behind a smile. Others didn't understand what she dealt with growing up in her lonely world and she wasn't willing to tell anyone her story. She suffered and experienced some great losses. She often wondered why she went through all she went through. Later learning, by the grace of God she can overcome. Throughout this story of Princess' life of what she considered hell, she found hope in Christ Jesus. The mask she wore to cover her issues of life were finally removed and the grace of God brought her all the way through!

Chapter 1

Isaiah 41:10 So do not fear, for I am with you; do not be dismayed, for I am your God. I will strengthen you and help you; I will uphold you with my righteous right hand.

It was a beautiful summer day, almost 100 degrees, so everyone was outside enjoying themselves, having water fights amongst friends. Deep inside, Princess felt like it was just an ordinary day for her. She sat inside of her room staring into space thinking, "Wow all of this beauty on the outside, and I feel dark, ugly, and blue on the inside." She found herself stuck in a state of depression.

She thought back, trying to figure out how she got to such a dark place. Then she's reminded of how she was hurt and left discouraged. Princess was dying on the inside, crying out for help with no one to turn to. There was no one there to ease the agonizing discomfort that she suffered with for years.

The laughter of the children broke her train of thought and brought her back to reality. She tried to focus on the positive image that was in front of her, unfortunately she was numb. Happiness did not reside in her life. How could she embrace a beautiful day knowing how hurt and broken she was?

Princess had a reason to feel the way she did at least that's what she thought. She never could understand why someone would do harm to a three-year-old child.

In the year 1997, the unthinkable happened. Princess had just began daycare where she was a carefree child playing with her doll, having make believe tea parties, doing what most three year old girls do. No one would have thought that an unsupervised visit to the bathroom with an older child would have snatched the first piece of happiness away from her. She was too young to understand the situation, to know what was happening at that moment in time. Princess did know that she was inside the bathroom for a long time alone with the older child. When she came out of the bathroom, her walk was different; it seemed as if something was hurting. Her teacher noticed and asked if she was alright. Tears began to stream down Princess' face.

"Are you in pain?" the teacher asked, placing her hand gently on her shoulder.

Princess shook her head and took hold of her hand leading her to the bathroom. Once inside, she pulled down her pants and pointed to the area where she was experiencing discomfort. Her teacher gasped, and stepped back.

"Princess…sweetheart…what happened to you?" Her face was flushed, and she could see her chest moving in and out fast.

Princess didn't know how to respond? She was only 3 years old and her panties were full of blood. Although, she didn't know how to express her feeling then, today she would say she was afraid. Scared that she was going to be in trouble or that she was somehow to blame for the blood in her panties.

This was the worst experience of her young life. She was embarrassed. Her teacher immediately called her mother. Princess's mother and aunt came running down to the daycare as the ambulance was coming down 20th street. They rushed her to Capital One Hospital for children and all she could do was cry with a loud scream. The blood was flowing in a constant flow out of her private area. It was the worst feeling ever. The event would leave Princess traumatized throughout most of her young life.

Being molested affected her entire life, to the point, she was afraid of being touched by anybody. Often times she would flashback to what happened and it caused her to temporarily 'lose her mind.' She always asked herself, *"Why me?"* It affected her mentally and physically. She felt like a loser, because out of all the kids at the daycare it had to happen to her. Why was she the target? She had to continue attending the daycare until she went to kindergarten at Hunter Elementary. Some of the kids at her daycare went there as well so it hurt her because she still had to be around the person who victimized her.

She was so terrified to sit next to that person in class. Her heart was beating 1000 beats a minute. Her mind was replaying that devastating day over and over again. One day the kid looked at her and she started to scream, "No, no!!!!"

The whole class looked at Princess as she lie on the desk holding her head and crying, not thinking that this is what she will have to deal with growing up.

She hated the fact that she was molested and it left her feeling rejected. Never could she imagine such a terrible thing. The loneliness only made it worse. When things happen to you, all you can do is try your best move to forward but it's much harder for a child without their mother and father standing with them.

Life for Princess didn't get any better. She had been through so many things she felt as if her life had been blown away. She felt as if no one ever loved her.

Rejection is like not being accepted. Being rejected is the one of the worst things a girl could experience. By the age of 10, Princess felt as if she was dying; there were times when she looked around and couldn't find anyone but her grandparents. She was like an angel without their wings, lost. It seemed as if she was raising herself. Princess's daddy was never around and her older siblings didn't really show her any attention. Her mother was nowhere to be found most of the time; leaving Princess alone to cry herself to sleep.

Being alone all the time caused her mind to play tricks on her. She began to hear noises and see shadows from the corner of her eye. She didn't know it then, but later in life she would learn, this was the enemy placing the spirit of fear in her life.

She would come home from school and lock herself in her room. One day she sat on her bed thinking about the dark places and how rejection played a tremendous part that caused her to stray away from GOD. She never knew that physically this would become a strong effect on her life. All she could think about was how her future would look having no one by her side, to back her up or assist her through her journey.

Princess didn't have anyone to call on but her grandparents, she was able to talk to them about anything. Most of her anger was with the ones who had actually rejected, abandoned, molested, and bullied her, but mostly with herself. She had to figure out what she was going to do because her head was turning in circles and she couldn't take it anymore. The pain was getting worse every day.

She started reading scriptures that her grandmother used to read to her. Isaiah 41:10 became her comfort scripture. Though she didn't really understand the scriptures, she felt like they would help ease the pain sometimes.

Chapter 2

Psalms 27:10 – When my father and my mother forsake me, then the LORD will take me up.

As Princess continued to feel like things in her life were getting worse, all she could think about was how her mother and father abandoned her as a child. She didn't have enough strength to get over being hurt. Her mother loved to be in the streets hanging with her friends, her father was never around. Her parents loved to party. It bothered Princess that her parents would prefer to be in the streets rather be home with her. Their lack of interest caused a void between parents and child. They never understood her, but how could they if they weren't around. They didn't know her; they just knew that she was their child.

She found refuge with her grandparents. They were all she had at the end of the day. She remembers having to stand alone at the bus stop in the mornings waiting for the school bus. She secretly envied the other children who had parents, or someone who cared about them standing in the rain, heat, cold, or any other obstacle with them.

Princess was extremely lost without a mother, and her deepest desire was a strong mother-daughter bond. She desired the TV relationships where mothers & daughters go shopping together; sit on a canopy bed painting each other nails, talking about boy crushes or the mother who was there to pick up the pieces when her best friend stabbed her in the back.

She wanted a father that would scare her future boyfriend when it was time to take her out on a date. A father who would teach her how to ride a bike or the one who would tell her that she was the most beautiful girl in the world. After a while she just wanted to give up on life. It seemed like everything was falling apart. But there was something in her that was telling her not to worry. Everything would be just fine.

Princess usually came home to an empty house when she returned from school. Instead of her mother greeting her with an afternoon snack, asking her how her day was, and if she had any homework; she was at her friend's house over on 45th street. Princess always went to see if her mother was there. Faith and Hope would always lie and tell her that her mother went to the store somewhere. Her mom was trying to hide certain stuff from her, as if she didn't know that she smokes and drinks with her friends. All the stuff that she did really didn't bother Princess. She could still do her thing; she just wanted a little time with her. She wanted to be as, or more important than the things she did when she was with Faith and Hope.

Princess was a young girl in need of answers. Things were changing in her life and she needed her mother's guidance. Instead she would blow Princess off like a leaf that falls from a tree. Sometimes she wouldn't be out with her friends; she would be in the same house with her, ignoring her as if she wasn't there. She was most likely too tired from partying or not in the mood to be bothered with Princess, her own daughter. When she would ask her for money she would always have to wait for the first of the month when her check would come. She didn't like the fact that when she asked her mother for money, Princess had to wait but when her mother wanted to go party, she didn't have to wait until the first of the month.

She never got the chance to wear name brand stuff like the other kids in her neighborhood. Their mothers received their first of the month checks too but they didn't look like her. She went to school looking a hot mess. The only thing her mother could think about was herself and pleasing her friends.

Princess flashed back to a memory when her mother decided to call her out of her name. If that wasn't bad enough she degraded her and said that she wouldn't make it in life. It was like she lived to make Princess' life a living hell. She didn't understand why. Princess didn't do anything to her mother. She didn't ask to be here. Those words broke her down instantly because she would never think that her own mother would call her out of her name and wish failure upon her. She just couldn't go through with it after being called a "B." That tore her apart. She never would've thought her own mother would go that far.

At that moment, she just had to walk away because she wanted to punch her mother, Hazel in her face. Yes, at that point she was not her mom, she was Hazel. Princess had been called a "B" before but coming from her mother, it damaged her mind. At that moment, Princess realized Hazel did not respect her as her daughter. She immediately ran upstairs to her room and crawled up into a ball as the tears rolled down her face. She felt hopeless because her mother didn't love her. It was like she was just a random girl on the streets of Bronx, New York.

Princess mom loved to talk about her bad with her friends because Princess always acted out in school. Hazel never showed her any love. She felt like her mom betrayed her. Because of Hazel, people looked at Princess differently. She just couldn't believe that a mother would do such a thing like that to her daughter; she was so ashamed and didn't want any bother out of her for a while.

Sometimes she tended to get extremely stressed out because abandonment sucks. It was a horrible thing to happen to a young girl like

Princess. Horrible is an understatement. Princess slipped into a depressive state.

In Princess' mind no one ever loved her from the moment she was born. Her appearance was raggedy; uncombed hair, she looked very un kept. There was nothing soft and pretty about her. Whenever she asked her mother for anything she always complained that she was broke but had money for the specific things she liked or loved to do with her friends; beers, weed, and cigars. Often times she would even search around to try and scramble up money so she can get those things instead of trying to help out her daughter with something she needed. Princess felt like she was always in a mental war. All she could do was try to fight her way through the field of being beaten by those horrible words and actions her mother showed. She just doesn't get it, *"Why Me?"* Did she cause this to happen because she was born out of wedlock? She hated her life!

She wished that she could have had perfect parents or parents that at least cared. Her father treated her as if she wasn't even his child. He never came around or called her to wish her a happy birthday. Instead he would curse her out and tell her how much of a failure she was. He reminded her that she was nothing and would most likely end up in jail. His hate for her was not hidden. The thing was, she didn't do anything to him to deserve such vile treatment. A father was supposed to love and protect their little girls; at least that's what she thought. He had other things on his agenda; like hanging out in the streets with his friends. Partying was his concern. He would out all night so he could drink his liquor and smoke his marijuana, without even thinking about calling Princess to say hello or happy birthday. She always wanted to be a daddy's little girl but he never wanted any bother out of her.

Princess' heart began to melt. She was so hurt because all she wanted was her father. Although he was never truly there for her, in her mind he would change. When that didn't happen, she fell deeper intodepression. She went to school and acted out to the point she had to see a counselor. The people at her school couldn't understand why she behaved that way. They didn't know that no love from her dad, the rejection from her mother and the molestation damaged her.

Hazel ended up marrying Princess's siblings' father. Unlike Princess, they always had both of their parents. The heaviness from hurt caused her to want to be far away from everyone. Now she was withdrawing from reality. She longed to disappear off to another place where she wanted to die. She thought her father hated her guts and she thought he behaved that way because she was a spitting image of her mother.

Often times Princess sat in her backyard on the steps thinking to herself, what would they do if she was dead and gone? The pain she felt broke her down to the point she kept asking, *"Why Me?"* There had to be a reason for the hate. Was it jealousy? Was it because she really was pretty? She was a light skinned little girl. She started thinking people hated her for that, even her parents. She kept wishing she could have a new life with better parents. Her mother and father treated her like trash. She pondered if she should just run away because no one but her grandparents loved her.

I opened this part of Princess' story with that scripture because when all else fails; when it seems like your mother and father have forsaken you, Jesus will heal you. The Lord will hear all of your cries. When you have nobody else to lean on, Jesus will be there in the midst of your troubles. He will lift your head up and wipe every tear from your eyes. Without a mother or father there, God will step in the midst of your life and he will allow you to stand on his promises, raising you up to be a strong survivor.

Chapter 3

Jeremiah 30:17For I will restore you to health and I will heal you of your wounds,' declares the LORD, 'Because they have called you an outcast, saying: "It is Zion; no one cares for her." '

As the years went by Princess always had the feeling that her older brother and sister didn't like her. They made her feel like she was the outcast because she didn't share the same father as them. It seemed as if the love they had for one another was stronger than the love they had towards her, as if they didn't love her at all.

There was a situation during a Spring Break that remained relevant in her mind for many years. It was very nice outside that day. Princess asked her siblings, "Do you want to go outside and play?" There was a pause. Both children looked at Princess with their faces frowned. They scowled at her as if she had said something vile. She ran upstairs to the bathroom and locked herself inside. The hate filled expressions on their faces crushed her young soul. Why did they hate her? She sat in the corner of the small bathroom in a fetal position and cried. That moment left a scar, Princess' relations to her siblings was now centered on the hate she felt from them.

Princess' and her sister were 9 months apart. They didn't get along at all. Her sister didn't like nor cared about her. When Princess tried to play with her sisters toys she would shout, "Get your fat hands off my stuff! Get your own toys!" Her sister was rude with a nasty attitude and could care less about the way she made Princess feel. This made Princess sad. She would cry for days.

The kind of relationship that Princess had with her sister was terrible. Princess swore her sister hated her because she had long hair and was light skinned. The boys seemed to like Princess better as well. She would always taunt Princess saying, "You're a Smith, not a Johnson, so mommy is not your mommy." This reoccurring jeer was meant to insinuate that Princess was an adopted child. She knows now that she said those things only because she knew it would upset Princess.

The siblings' attitudes toward Princess, made her wonder if she left that home, would all of her troubles be gone?

Her father had favorites; he made it evident that it wasn't Princess. The way he praised her sister and did things for her made Princess envy her. His treatment or lack thereof of Princess angered her to the point that she hated her sister and wished she was dead. Yeah she regrets the words that she said but at that moment she was hurt. Princess continued to wonder *"Why Me?"* Princess thought sisters were supposed to be like best friends.

Time after time, she'd go into her grandparent's room and find herself sitting on their bed crying thinking, no one loves me. Sisters should love each other but instead Princess' sister hated her. The only thing Princess could do was try her best to stay away and find someone that would take her in their arms and love her like a little sister.

Princess' mind was torn into pieces; she didn't know what to do. All she could say is, *"Why Me?"* Crying every night without a shoulder to lean on, everyone hated her. The depression started to set in again and she started to get sick and tired of people treating her that way. Her darkness seemed like it was never coming to an end. Did she do something wrong? She longed for someone that loved her.

She already knew that her sister didn't like her. Her brother began to tell her outright, "Get away, I hate you".

Those words were so hurtful she wished someone would come and rescue her. It was like someone hit her with a stick in her back. She couldn't believe he'd really said, "I hate you." Her brother often told her she thought that she was better than everybody because she was the smart one out of the bunch.

Princess and her brother were playing in the living room and he didn't want her to play with his basketball court so she knocked it down and broke it. She was so angry because they never allowed her to play with their toys knowing she had very few of her own. He pushed her down onto the couch and started doing wrestling moves on her. She was afraid that he was going to hurt her. Princess just couldn't understand, *"Why Me?"*

There were times when she would make attempts at kindness toward him and he would simply push her away. There was an incident when she was inside the kitchen trying to make some tuna fish when her brother saw her hand get stuck inside the can and laughed. He then ran to get their sister so she could join in on making fun of Princess. Princess yanked her hand out fast, not caring if she hurt herself. Her index finger was split open and once she saw the blood all she could do was scream to the top of her lungs. She frantically grabbed for a paper towel while her brother and sister watched laughing. "Haha. We hate you anyway; I hope you bleed to death!" *"Why Me?"* She asked herself that question repeatedly. The words they said to her were so terrifying; she just couldn't help but cry. "Princess wanted her life to be perfect, so she could be the girl she desired to be and live to see happiness.

Princess wasn't your typical girl, she always had a love for basketball. Most of her friends were boys so she picked up some of their characteristics. Her brother would tell her that she was a boy and that she looked gay. He'd constantly tell her she should've been a boy, because she would always do what boys do. Yes, Princess was a tomboy but she wasn't gay. The truth was she never enjoyed the traits that her female peers displayed; she didn't have time for fake friends who gossiped behind her back. She was teased so much for her tomboyish behavior, she had become accustomed to being called a "dyke" and "gay." She heard it so much that she too began to wonder if she liked females in that way. Those words hurt Princess. She felt like she was bleeding on the inside; no one could see what she was going through. Overall, the life she had with her siblings was not the best. Compared to most sibling relationships, theirs would be considered shameful in the public eye.

Princess would soon learn that God would restore her and heal her wounds. She was not alone, He had not forgotten her, and soon the answers to her cries would arrive.

Chapter 4

Matthew 5:10-11 Blessed are they which are persecuted for righteousness' sake: for theirs is the kingdom of heaven. Blessed are ye, when men shall revile you, and persecute you, and shall say all manner of evil against you falsely, for my sake.

Princess was a true victim of bullying. She would be bullied every day in school and at home. People would ask how she was holding up; she would lie and say she was well, knowing she was slowly dying inside. If you haven't been bullied and don't know what it feels like well here is one word to describe it PAINFUL! It hurts, causing you to feel depressed, wanting to stay in the house away from people, starve yourself, and just think about jumping off of a bridge. It feels like you have no one to talk to. The truth is there was someone to talk to, GOD! However Princess was unaware with what she was dealing with.

Being bullied takes control of your body because you tend to get low self-esteem, look at yourself different, become a little disrespectful or just try to at least understand why you are being bullied as a little girl. By this time, she was in the fifth grade and it was the first day of school. Princess was tiny when she was in kindergarten; as the years had gone by she had picked up weight. Her peers started to make fun of her being overweight at such a young age. Being teased in such a way made her become delusional. In her eyes, she wasn't fat, she was thick. Princess didn't think that her weight would make a difference in her life. Her friends were supposed to accept her for who she was, not what she looked like. Princess soon found out that was not how things worked.

Bullying can mess up a whole life. It can cause you to lose your mind when you have friends that stab you in the back. Boys that once thought you were cute now laugh in your face. *"Princess, you ugly and stupid, looking just like Barney!"* they would taunt her.

The bullying Princess suffered through, caused hate to form in her heart, not just any hate, but malice. She wanted to physically hurt those who tormented her. There was a group of girls Princess hung out with and they all picked on her as well. Jorie, she was the ring leader of the group that consisted of Jazzman, Sierra and Rebecca. These girls would say things like, *"Hey Princess, you too fat to play with us. You know it's the truth because you can't even run."* Or, *"You just fat for nothing, girl. You not even cute, that's why Jose and Darnell don't like you anymore."* There was no filter when they talked to her. Princess began to feel as if she just wasn't anybody. They had no regard for her feelings.

As the school year continued, she found herself aggravated daily. The words were doing more damage than her young mind could cope with. She was broken, alone, and depressed. There was no double Dutch, tag playing, or sliding board activities at recess for her. She would be in the corner crying trying to figure out, *"Why me?"* She couldn't understand why every time something is going on with her no one cared about her hurt and pain. It's like she was stuck in a hole with no one to help her out.

Although the bullying hurt, she didn't allow it to stop her from progressing. She had received Honor Roll and Perfect Attendance She was determined not to allow her weight to stop her from reaching a great goal heading towards a greater future.

By the time Princess had graduated from Elementary school she was now entering the sixth grade when it felt like she was in a dream. The bullying leveled up to the extreme. The girls Jorie, Jazzman, Sierra, and Rebecca also attended J. Higgs Middle school with Princess and it brought back a lot of memories. During classes, they would all gang up on her. They insulted her to no end. They teased her for having good grades, suggesting she thought she was better than them because of her accomplishments.

The situation at school caused her to go into a deeper state of depression than what she had been already experiencing. Her home life was an issue. School had once been her escape, now she was to the point that she didn't want to be there either. She would try to get out of going by saying she was physically ill. In some respects, she was ill, the mental abuse made her weary causing her to lose focus and feel drained.

When Princess returned to school. The girls thought it would be funny to mock her making loud sounds as if she was a beast walking down the halls. Jorie attended the same math class as Princess. Princess had a pretty good handle on math, but Jorie had no clue what the teacher was talking about. Princess tried to help Jorie with her math so that she would be able to understand how to do the work but Jorie didn't want her too. It was awful to continue to walk the school hallways knowing that people don't like you just for who you are and what you do that makes everything fall apart.

After enduring the bullying so long it had gotten so heavy on Princess's mind she couldn't take it anymore. There were times when all Princess wanted to do was knock somebody out and continue to get sent to detention so she wouldn't have to deal with all those girls talking, laughing, and writing notes about her during class. Princess had to save herself so that she could maintain an excellent education. Many people had so much hatred for Princess simply because she was smart and willing to help others.

As the year went by, it was like things were becoming a murder scene in Princess' life because she couldn't take all the hurt and the suffering any more. She wished that those girls would just stop spreading rumors around the school so she could live her life in peace.

Princess tried out for the basketball team and for the band. She became a part of both. Princess was very talented which made her enemies dislike her more. Basketball was Princess's dream. She wanted to be in the WNBA when she got older because basketball was her favorite sport. She enjoyed playing. In band class, Princess played the drums and the clarinet. She favored the drums. After basketball season was over and band ended, Princess really didn't have anything else to do but she did try out for the wrestling team and made it. She ended up quitting because she was teased by the boys on the wrestling team.

Princess began to become discouraged again. She wanted to give up on school. Bullying was affecting her life and the way she lived outside of her home. One week it was school pride. Princess was happy because she loved to wear her school colors during color war between the grades. Princess walked into the school that Friday morning with her color on, which was red. She was all decked out; she had a nice red polo shirt on, with some cute skinny leg jeans and some red and white Converse like sneakers. Princess was sitting downstairs in the cafeteria getting ready to get breakfast and her morning was starting off great. Great until, that is, people begin to crowd around her and laugh and mock her because she had some Air Walk "fake" Converse on. Princess took off into the bathroom hiding inside the stall, wanting to hang herself because she'd had enough. But, something stopped her, she began to think about all her dreams and goals she wanted to fulfill as she got older.

Princess stayed in the bathroom until it was time to go to first period. Princess put her earphones in and turned them up loud so she didn't have to hear the people back there laughing at her shoes. Princess had to listen to music so that she could ease all her pain instead of ending her life. As the day went on she started to feel better.

The school day was over and it was now time to go home. As Princess was getting on the bus someone threw a rock at her, hitting her right on the head. Finally, Princess had enough and she darted at Jorie, Jazzman, Sierra and Rebecca and started to fight all of them. She was over being bullied the whole school year and it was now time to let it all out.

Later that night, she was preparing for the school dance. She wore a dress that was royal blue and gold with some cute high heels the same color.

She thought she looked beautiful. Her date, James had arrived. His attire matched hers and they went to take pictures.

Princess's grandparents took her to the dance and when they pulled up to the place all eyes were on their Silver Lincoln. People were wondering who was getting out of this fancy car. James got out first then went around opening the door for Princess. The girls were amazed at what she looked like and still were jealous because she looked so pretty. Her outfit was on point and decked out. She had the time of her life despite the horror she had endured earlier that day. She realized if she had ended her life she would have never had such a wondrous memory to look back on.

When people persecute you and speak evil of you, God will always be there for your sake. You have to remember, you will have some enemies along the way during your life but blessed are those who will get help from God during every trial and tribulation. Your worst enemy can be someone you love or people that may be jealous of you. However, God has the last say so and He will be with you forever. Because of God you are fearfully and wonderfully made. He will always be your present help in the time of trouble.

Chapter 5

It was now time to start the ninth grade Princess couldn't imagine how it would be. She couldn't help to think, she would finally be reaching a dream; graduation. During her first year of high school it was a little rough to the point it felt like she was replaying middle school all over again. She had to think to herself like when is all of this going to end. Why won't this bullying stuff ever stop? It was like someone was trying to drive her to her grave. Princess was fed up with all of that bullying It was almost daily she'd run into the girl's bathroom, crying her eyes out in those dirty stalls. She never knew that this would be the type of things that she would have to deal with when it comes to living her life.

Princess' freshman year of high school she tried out for the field hockey team. She thought if she stayed active she could lose weight and if she lost weight maybe the bullying would slow down. People on the team didn't really like to be around her because she was great at field hockey.

Her talent was building up her confidence, which was making her name great and a lot of people thought she was doing it all for show.

Princess was afraid of what people would think because she was always being judged throughout her life. Princess had to focus on herself while in the ninth grade. She couldn't allow her bullies to knock her off the square because she was trying to reach her dream. Losing weight was her main goal because she was tired of people criticizing her and calling her names. As the season came to an end for field hockey Princess was named one of the star players on the team. Princess grades were on point, except for gym class. She would get at least a C because some days she would have trouble running the pacer tests which caused her to get a low grade.

During her gym period, Princess would always focus on shooting hoops. A group of girls came crowding around her and started to push her around. Princess'mind begins to go around and around, her thinking was getting intense to the point she had to sit down before she passes out onto the gym floor. It was almost the end of the day and Princess was getting ready to go home, but she was so stressed out wishing everyone would stop teasing her about the way she looked. Princess *thought* she was a beautiful 14-year-old but every time she looked in the mirror she felt like it should have cracked because of the horrible things people said about her. Princess started holding on to the horrible things people said.

Princess started to believe that she was ugly indeed. She avoided taking pictures for class assignments. Princess started to think about basketball to take her mind off the ugliness that people tended to throw in her face. She was excited basketball season was almost here!

Princess was super excited because basketball was her favorite sport and she loved playing the game. She felt it would keep her motivated on the right track towards her dream. Other girls in her class Jessica and Yasmin would tease her and laugh saying that she couldn't play basketball because she was too overweight. So, as she was in gym class for the next couple of weeks, Princess begin to grab a basketball and dribble up and down the court to prove that she was everything that the basketball team needed. She wanted to let Jessica and Yasmin know that there is no shame in her game and she was the best at basketball.

Princess was leaving her last class, getting ready to catch the 3:00 school bus when Jessica and Yasmin ran up behind her. They taunted her saying, "Hey fatty! Wednesday basketball season starts but you're too big to make the team anyway. The coaches don't want a freshman like you playing on their team." Princess remained quiet and rushed to her bus. Even on the ride home from school she was still getting bullied and that's when the suicidal and depressed thoughts came back and Princess couldn't take it anymore.

Even other kids begin to yell in her face and call her all types of names. She sat in her seat wondering, *"Why me."* Princess's sister, Myrtle, didn't even care. She would join right in and it truly hurt Princess heart because she never thought that her sister would go against her at school.

Princess just sat down in the front of the bus all the way home from school. She would try to listen to music so that she could take her mind off of all that yelling and name calling in her ear and behind her back. Princess was filled with hurt and an undying pain. She didn't understand what was going on with her life. It felt like everything was falling apart and all she wanted to do was lay down and die. She had no idea that her sister would be sitting there entertaining that crap and it truly upset her to the max where she just wanted to explode. While Princess was getting off the bus those ignorant school kids thought it was a joke to trip her, causing her to fall on her face and slightly twist her right ankle. *"Why Me!"* She just couldn't understand. All she wanted to do was live a normal life like any other teenage girl. All of Princess things fell out of her hand and those kids begin to kick it all over into the street. Telling her to, "Go fetch fat girl, slide on your belly you seal." So she thought, "I should kill myself" but she thought about her future. She wanted to prove to naysayers that she will do great in life. The Lady Joy's Basketball Team would be her next accomplishment.

Before you knew it basketball season was about to start. Princess had already taken in so much heart ache and pain from bullying day after day. Princess put her focus on sports to let them know that she can do it just like everyone else can no matter how big or how small she was basketball material and will prove it all.

One day Princess had to press her way to school after staying up all night popping pill after pill to numb her mental pain. She didn't know how in the world she made it to school but now it was her time to shine. She had her hair done in these cute long poetic justice braids with her ripped jeans and fly shirt on. She thought she looked good. She went to first period and couldn't wait until the end of the day for basketball tryouts to begin. Princess remained focus during class time. As the day went by Jessica and Yasmin would say "Hey you biggie, are you're ready for b-ball tryouts?" Princess just looked at them and rolled her eyes. She was trying not to get distracted and think about how she tried to kill herself over them last night because they bullied her every single day.

After about three classes it was now time for lunch. Princess got a small salad with a slice of pizza for lunch. She was sitting by herself in a small corner watching a video on her phone about depression. Her mind was telling her to kill herself. She thought all the things that Yazmin and Jessica said and the fact that they hated her guts. During lunch Myrtle was about to fight. Princess didn't pay that any attention because her sister wasn't caring about her and her troubles. A teacher asked Princess to stop her sister from fighting. Princess told the teacher, "Tuh! That ain't my sister. I ain't stopping her from doing nothing." Princess wanted Myrtle to get beat up so bad. Myrtle is very mean and ignorant even to her own blood. Princess ended up stopping her sister from fighting so she wouldn't get expelled from school.

Princess went upstairs after lunch to her locker so that she could get her books for her next class and her music stuff for band. She started heading towards her math class when she sees those girls who were messing with her in the lunch room. They looked as if they were coming for Princess and she was ready to physically defend herself by any means necessary. They walked by just laughing. As she walked into her math class her teacher had changed her seat. Princess was able to get away from those bullies so they wouldn't bother her during class period. Even though she was sitting in the front, that didn't stop them from messing with her. Notes were being passed around the room about Princess. Her classmates were reading them, laughing and pointing fingers at her. She kept trying to focus on what the teacher was teaching until it was time for her next class period.

She walked down the hallway to band class, that was her favorite class because as she loved playing on the instruments. It allowed some of her stress and things that was hindering her throughout the day to come out during music. During band class she was very good at playing both the clarinet and snare drums. She enjoyed making music. Princess played those instruments very well and the sound was so profound and great. Well band class was now coming to an end and Princess started to put the instruments away. Next up was basketball tryouts so she proceeded to go to her locker so she could grab her pink bag for tryouts. It was now her time to shine on the court and prove to those girls that whatever they said about her being overweight was wrong. Princess went into the bathroom stall to change into her try out clothes. She put on her nice black basketball shorts, and white t-shirt that said "Fly Christian" on it. She also wore some nice gold and black Jordan's that someone gave her, on. She was now ready to take the court. Oh yeah don't forget about her cute colorful socks and glasses she wore so that she will be able to see better. Now it was time for her and the other girls to head out to the court and get ready to run some drills. After stretching she would be prepared for whatever it takes to make the Lady Joy's Girls Basketball team. The coaches split the girls up. Princess was a little bit nervous. She was on the same side as the girls who told her she wouldn't make the team.

She put all that she had into the tryouts and the coaches were impressed and they pushed her to the max because she never gave up. At the end of the tryouts it was now time to see who made the team and would start their first practice tomorrow after school. Princess never took her eyes off of her goals and dreams. Even if people thought she wouldn't make the team she would still strive to do her best. She ended up making the team. She made the Junior Varsity team. This was one of the best days of Princess' life. She set her mind to it and she did it! She was so good she even sometimes played with the Varsity girls during games and practices.

Those girls who doubted her made the freshman team. They weren't good enough for Junior Varsity. They didn't really put in too much effort in order to make the team. They thought it was just all fun and games. As she left the gym and headed to get dressed, the girls tried to fight her. That day she had really had enough. She was tired of the bullying. Princess physically defended herself. She held her own and wasn't afraid. They just stop fighting her and ran away.

While she was waiting on the after school bus, the gym was still open. She went inside and started to shoot around until 6 o'clock. She ran into those same girls and had to ride home with them on the bus. Princess became very irritated because they would still talk smack instead of leaving her alone. She ignored them. As soon as Princess got off the bus, she ran home. Princess went into the house and let her grandparents know that she had made the girls basketball team at school. They were very proud of her. Because she didn't allow others to make her think she wasn't going to make it.

Now it was time for the very first basketball practice. She was totally ready to get this season started and prepare for her future because Princess felt like she was reaching towards greatness. During the first practice there was different drills that they ran and it was hard for her to catch up to some of the Varsity girls when it came to running but they continued to push Princess and she never gave up. Basketball is her favorite sport and she enjoyed playing the game. Basketball allowed her to let out all of her feelings with being depressed and having major suicide thoughts. After the Saturday practice she felt a little bit better. As some games went by she really didn't get that much time to play because sometimes she would get nervous. She sometimes would have to be on the court with those same girls who teased and laughed at her. Princess would have flashbacks about how those girls were saying she was ugly and big and unable to be a part of the team.

Princess thought her coaches would show a lot of favoritism to other girls on her team. She would get upset thinking that it wasn't fair. During the season she had scored at least 12 points a game with about 5 blocks and maybe 1 steal. She never lost focus even though she didn't get that much playing time. She would always try her best to focus on the court and keep her mind on the game so that her team could come out with a win. By the time the middle of basketball season came around Princess and the Lady Joy's was on their way to the state championship. She was inspired by this star player who was a senior. They called her "Jones" Jones began to push Princess to the max because she believed in her. Princess was inspired by Jones because in her 11th grade year she got hurt and couldn't finish the season out. But she came back her senior year pushing harder and she snapped. It provoked Princess to never give up on the game. Jones would always say "Look out for the assist, go in strong to the basket, you're unstoppable, girl!" She was Princess' motivator and would always have her back. So that year the Lady Joy's made it to the championship game and ended up coming out with a 75-50 win, that was the best night ever. Jones finished strong with 5 three points and 5 assists and Princess ended the game with a double double. She finished the season out with a bang and accomplished so many things in the end, because of her coaches and Jones pushing her on the sideline at the beginning of the season.

She had an amazing basketball season but now it was time to finish out the year and get ready for a fantastic summer. There was still some bullying going on but she did gain a little bit of respect after all. She never allowed her issues to cause her to give up, she succeeded in the end. It was the last day of school and she was ready to go home and start her summer. She received Honor Roll once again and couldn't wait to go home and show her parents. She was happy about school being over but was once again haunted with the fact that no one but her grandparents would be proud of her accomplishments that year. She tried to imagine having parents that would be excited about her accomplishments, even rewarding her with money or something special. Reality brought Princess to depression again. All that she had accomplished, she still had no support from those she wanted it from so bad; her parents and siblings. She wanted to die. Now, she dreaded the summertime coming; getting teased about her outfits because of her fat legs and big arms. Princess hated that and couldn't stand going outside on hot and sunny days. She would just sit in the house and watch TV. She had got sick and tired of people with their negative thoughts and ignorant words that she realized if she heard one more thing she would end her life.

She continued with school as usual. She received excellent grades and did great in basketball and band. The bullying continued. She experienced one horrific situation after another. Towards the end of the year things changed slightly. She received a letter in the mail stating she could attend a new school next year. She was accepted to a Vo-tech school. She could choose Philips or APC Tech. She really wanted to go to Philips but APC Tech was her mother's choice. She could not wait for the new school year to come. She figured things had to be better. She was getting a fresh start.

September 1, 2010, she was super excited to start her new school. She got up with a positive attitude ready to put on her new uniform and all white Nikes. Her outfit was everything and it matched her style but as she got to the bus stop people were looking at her giggling because she didn't have LeBron James or Kevin Durant sneakers on. She got on the bus and sat in the front because she didn't want them to clown her anymore. She put in her headphones and blasted the music the entire ride. A new school but no change. *"Why me?"* she thought.

The bullying continued when she arrived to school. She was in the cafeteria and a group of girls walked by and started to make sounds and gestures as if she had a foul odor. She went and got her breakfast and sat by herself to look over her schedule so she could find her first class. It took her some time but she ended up finding her class, though she was little late. When she entered the room there was so many laughs going up and people saying things like, "OMG look at her fat self." She felt hopeless. She felt like she was back at her old school all over again. Again she felt that she couldn't take it. She was so depressed. She slept through her first class. She was corrected for sleeping in class but her temper was so intense that her response made the teacher kick her out of class.

She was headed to detention for the first time and just sat there the whole class period with her head on the desk crying. After about three class periods she wanted to go home and hang herself. She thought her life was over and this bullying would never stop.

During her lunch period, she sat alone at a table and listened to music while eating. She figured that no one liked her or cared about her. That is, until one day she met an awesome counselor who treated her like a queen and lifted her up with encouraging words and a comforting hug. The counselor's name was, Mary. Ms. Mary was a lifesaver. Two girls walked by and asked Ms. Mary "Why are you talking to her? She is going to eat you! Can't you see! She just big and disgusting." She did her best to ignore them.

It was almost the end of the day and Princess was so ready to go home. She spent the rest of her day inside her shop, which was, Academy of Finance and Business. She did her work in silence. She didn't want to hinder anyone else since she was way too ugly and too fat to be around anyone. A few hours later that class was finally over. The bell rang, and it was time to head to the bus so she could go home. She was so upset because it felt like her whole day was a disaster and she never wanted to come back to the school again. Later that night she went home and started to write a suicide note.

Princess had enough and couldn't take any more of the depression or bullying. She just wanted to end her life. She went down stairs into the kitchen and got a knife and some rope she found so she could hang herself. She locked herself in the room, and at that moment the tears started to roll down her face. She was either going to slice her wrist, tie the rope around her neck to hang herself, or take a whole bottle of pills...either way, she was ending it all. She heard someone calling her name to come down and eat but she didn't answer. Her grandmother, Lorraine, came up and knocked on the door. She cried, continuing to slice her wrist. She passed out onto the floor. Lorraine couldn't get into the room and Princess wasn't answering, so she took a butter knife and unlocked it. She found Princess lying on a pile of clothes with blood coming from her wrist and an empty pill bottle lying next to her.

Lorraine was devastated and didn't know what to do. She yelled for someone to call the ambulance. She sat on the floor and held Princess' head in her lap, decreeing and declaring over her life that she shall live and not die. Her sister and brother came running up the steps because they heard Lorraine praying. They looked at her holding Princess in her arms and the blood. They burst into tears. Princess starting coming to, coughing up blood and mucus asking, "What is going on? What happened?" She wasn't sure if she had died or not. She looked around and saw her family crying over her pleading the blood of Jesus, but she still had no clue what was going on. What she tried to do was unsuccessful. She thought, "I couldn't even end my life right." She looked up at her grandmother and noticed an unexplainable glow about her. Princess eyes were fixed her grandmothers face and her ears were fixed on what her grandmother was saying. Her face was peaceful and she was singing praises to God, thanking Him for answering her prayers to save Princess' life. Princess was amazed at the peace her grandmother had in the midst of all this chaos and how could she possibly be giving God praises during this

Her grandparents would often tell her there is someone named Jesus that can help you get through all of your hurt and pain. God wouldn't allow her to die. He brought her back. She didn't understand why but she started thinking, maybe she does have some sort of purpose.

Chapter 6

Often times Princess would have flashbacks of all the terrible things the world had done to her. She would replay her most traumatic moments. Princess could never understand why people criticized and degraded her, her entire life. It was like she would never be able to cope with the pain that she felt every moment of her life. People still bullied and talked about her from time to time. They'd make fun of her clothes. Especially when she wore things like FUBU. Telling her it stood for Fat, Ugly, Black and Uncomfortable. She was fearful entering junior year of high school. She was haunted by her sophomore year. She made up in her mind that she would get her education and try not to focus on how she was being treated day to day. She told herself the way people treat her is not important. She tried to hold on to her success with basketball as her motivation to push through

Princess was still in a state of depression, not wanting to live, but she had some things she needed to accomplish to reach her goals. She was extremely stressed and had developed a bad attitude because she was over school at the moment.

That is, until she met her best friends Allison and Bianca. They treated her great and with sincerity. They showed her respect and allowed her to express her feelings with them when she needed to.

Princess's junior year was a time she got to show her special talent on and off the court again. It made her feel special that she actually had friends who were for her and not against her. Junior year was a major part in her Princess's life, because she was closer to her breaking point and before she knew it, her senior year would have arrived.

She was in a shop that allowed her to build some background and plan out her short and long-term goals. Princess was even able to go on trips because some projects required her to travel and compete in Dover for a major competition. She was very excited and always wanted to do something great so that the people who laughed at her would see her potential and success.

Princess was very intelligent but had a nasty attitude because of what she was dealing with throughout her life. Half way into the junior year she got straight A's for the first two marking periods. Princess was proud of herself because she never believed that she could make it in life through all of her hurt and criticism. Nevertheless, through it all, she still gave it her best and fought.

November 15, 2012, it was now time for her to try out for sports again. She was still very depressed and had an unworthy state of mind. But she refused to give up the fight and believed in herself with all her might that she would make the team regardless of anything that was going on during class, in the hallways, on the school bus, or at home. Basketball was her sport and during tryouts she gave it her all and made the team. Her coaches, Paul and Jenny, helped her along the way because they saw how much effort she was putting in.

After Princess made the team she was ready to conquer, it was her dream goal to make it this far so that she could accomplish something and end up playing basketball in college.

During the basketball season, Princess met friends, on and off the court, who loved the game just like she did. Life tried to shut her down but her game would never be affected, because it's the way she gets all of her hurt and pain out and behind her when she hits the court. She did her best to score and win the games. The common saying at the time was, "GO HARD OR GO HOME." Princess always went hard because that was her life.

When her grandparents passed away, Princess became more depressed and again wondered, *"Lord why me?"* Princess couldn't understand why God would take them if they were her motivators and support. Princess would cry and scream, it felt like no one could answer or help. She would begin to cut herself, smoke weed, drink alcohol, take pills, and beat on herself. She didn't care anymore, she wanted to be with her grandparents in heaven so that she would have some peace and wouldn't have to worry about anyone bullying her, making her feel like an outcasted, rejected, bastard.

Smoking weed became Princess's best friend. She would smoke every day, all day after school and on the weekends. But one night there was a voice that caused her to pause in the middle of her smoking saying, "Daughter you won't see your grandparents this way; if you live in sin. I promise you, if you give your life to Me, then all of your problems will be in My hands and I will cast them away."

Princess didn't know what the voice was so she kept smoking and drinking her drink because she didn't care anymore, she was over life and just wanted to be taken out.

One year later it was now time to enter the 12th grade. Princess was still in a state of not caring and would still do her own thing. Princess was in class looking up ways to end her life. She had tried many things but couldn't understand why it would never work. It was like her life was worth fighting for, whatever she tried it didn't kill her.

Every night she would go home smoke her weed back to back, sip on her drink, and start slicing up her wrists and sometimes popping pills.

The next day she would have a bad hangover while in school, sitting there looking stupid because she had no clue of what was going on with her life. It was like Princess had lost herself along the way and her life was headed down the wrong path.

Princess would go to church every Sunday but she wasn't really saved. She would jump and shout, even be a door keeper or usher from time to time but she wasn't really saved. She would only have attended church because that seemed like a place where she could act out. She didn't realize that church was keeping her in the midst. It was somehow fulfilling her and the prayers was shielding and protecting her from the enemy. The more she went to church, things started changing. From the inside, out.

Princess was in school one week and she felt different, it was like she had bounced back into reality. She began to do excellent work and later that day her shop teacher let her know that she had an interview coming up. She knew that she would be something great but felt in her spirit that she was an unworthy and unfit person, even if she still did what she was told while in school. Her life was pitiful at home; she was doing a lot of dirt and didn't understand why a company would call her in for an interview.

Senior year was something that should be accomplished in every child's life. Princess thought she wasn't going to make it, because she was living in sin and unworthy to God. There was a time that she could be taken out in sin and not make it to graduate high school. Princess was a fantastic student and she did allow her actions to cause her to get into trouble, but she had tamed it down a little bit. She wanted to get an amazing career and make her way to college next year with wonderful scholarships.

A few months later it was time for Princess to start her new job. She would be an intern at a bank called Learning Bank of Christians. She really was proud of herself because she knew that to maintain and finish school she needed to get a job. So, after she had got the job, things begin to shift in her life. She began to stop smoking and drinking and would say that she should live and not die. Princess had some insight on how her future would be, because she would constantly be reminded that she was great and that there are people who need to hear her testimony.

On April 8th, 2013 Princess attended a youth service and she felt the power of God. She began crying out to Him and gave her life back to Him; it felt like her whole life was changed completely. Later that day, all she could think about is how in the world could something happen like this to a girl that has so much stuff going on in her life. Why would someone want to help her out? But she had to come to herself and said that there is a greater anointing on her, so without God she would be so miserable and could die. It was by the grace and mercy of God that, when Princess tried to take her life, it wouldn't work all she could say is, *"Why Me!"*

The reason was because someone needed to hear her story on how she made it through. Her testimony on how unworthy she felt she was, and how God saw fit to save her life, so that she could continue to conqueror in Him and see her grandparents again. She was so amazed that God would see fit to save a life like hers.

Princess worked hard at her job, she loved it and could always talk to her co-workers about school. They would uplift and encourage her. When she got to that job, she was a little nervous, but as they showed her love, she knew that she was in good hands. She had accomplished a lot of stuff and learned new things at that job, which would help her along the way with an amazing future for as a Business Professional. By the next four months, it was almost time for Princess's senior year to come to an end. She couldn't play basketball her senior year because of work but she did end a great school year with straight A's and

B's and a 3.5 GPA. It was a hard life but she felt she had finally made it.

It was the day before prom and Princess didn't have anything to wear. She began to panic because she was running for prom queen and wanted to look flawless. Princess went out and found a dress that was one of a kind. She wore a cute hot pink and silver dress with sparkles, it was super-duper sexy and her hair was sharp. She was getting ready to get her makeup done and then she would get dressed for her night. Princess was going to prom by herself and she looked great.

She arrived at the prom and it was almost time to walk the runway to see who won prom queen. As she prepared to walk down the steps there was an announcement cheering her on. She looked very pretty in her pink, she just couldn't resist stopping and pausing with a pose and Dab dance. It was now time to call the name for the winner. Princess had her fingers cross, she really wanted to win. It would be one of her biggest accomplishments, along with graduating high school, and attending college to play basketball. Before you knew it, they screamed out the winner and it was Princess! She started to cry and jump up in the air because she couldn't believe that anyone voted for her. All the times she thought no one liked her. Well, she must have won them over when the end of the school year came.

She was so honored that she was prom queen and she realized that maybe some people do like her and that made it an amazing night. Prom night was the best night of Princess's life. She couldn't believe that she was prom queen, but in her mind, she still would think that she was an ugly person with a huge body. There were two more days left until graduation and Princess was ready to walk across the stage that was going to be another accomplishment of her life. She would finally get to make her grandparents proud even though they weren't physically there, she felt they still looked after her.

Princess made sure she never gave up. When all hell was breaking loose she continued to press through all her pain. The day had come where should could finally wear her all white cap and gown to show that she finally made it through every storm. As she was getting ready to be seated she looked over into the crowd and saw all her family and tears started to roll down her face. Her grandparents were not there to see her walk across the stage and accept her diploma. It was time for Princess's row to be called, she heard her family begin to scream, "Go, Princess, go!" She was getting ready to approach the stage when they announced her name, "Princess Leilani Smith!" She started to cry walking across the stage thrusting her hand holding the diploma in the air towards her family. She couldn't stop crying because she didn't understand how she made it this far in life with all of the mental issues she had while growing up. Graduation was over and Princess went to take pictures with her family and friends. She cried tears of joy because she had not given up, but pressed beyond measure and made it. Class of 2013! Yes, she did it!

Princess was a virgin until the age of 19 because she wanted to live her life right and wait until she got married. This way there was no distractions to her goals of earning a degree in Business while playing basketball.

Princess was on her way up. She had gotten accepted into an awesome college with a full scholarship and she would also be able to play basketball. She went with other girls to Penn State Lehigh Valley to tour the compass and sign enrollment papers. School would start in August of 2013 and Princess was ready. In fact, Princess was ready to start a new career and finally get to do what she'd dreamed since a young age. It was like she was almost headed to the WNBA.

Princess was still in church. She didn't understand why God helped her get this far with all of the things that she did throughout her life. After church, she had gone to hang out with a friend and they were smoking weed and drinking. She was ashamed because they wanted to celebrate her accomplishment so she couldn't turn them down. Princess was just trying to fit in with the crowd and ended up doing something that night that she regretted. It might have caused her whole life to fall apart once again.

Two months went by and Princess got really sick out of the blue, she couldn't keep anything down. She didn't know what was going on with her body. Princess was constantly using the bathroom and sleeping all the time. Her boyfriend called her later that day to inform her that he needed a "break".

At that moment, she knew that she was unworthy and God wasn't happy because of what she had done. It was like she threw her dream away because now she had lost her virginity and she was still in church. She felt like her life was ruined because sex was a sin and she was still smoking weed and drinking Peach Vodka. In spite of her hidden lifestyle, she was still giving God praise in church. She was ready to give up everything because now her life wasn't pleasing to God anymore. She felt unworthy doing what she did while in church. Princess's body begin to get even thicker than before. She didn't know why her shape was changing. Dimples were forming in her back and her waist expanded. Princess couldn't remember if they had used any protection or not because she wasn't in her right mind but she had a feeling that she was pregnant and knew that God wouldn't be pleased. She started having sex and now she could possibly be having a baby at a young age.

The opening scripture to this chapter identifies that if you believe in God, He will never leave you nor forsaken you, but you will have everlasting life. You just have to put your faith in God and trust Him that He will see you all the way through every trial and tribulation. Keep believing in God stand on his promises because He gave His only son for your sins and mines so that we would have eternal life. Just love on God and even if it feels like you're going to die in the storm He will guide you all the way until you make it out victorious.

Chapter 7

Psalms 61:1-2 Hear my cry, O God; attend unto my prayer. From the end of the earth will I cry unto thee, when my heart is overwhelmed: lead me to the rock that is higher than I.

A few months later, Princess was still getting sick and didn't understand why her body was feeling like it was. She was weak and all she wanted was to sleep. So, Princess had taken two tests to see if she was with child and they both came back negative. She had started to have a lot of pain in her stomach and her nose was spreading. She thought the change was happening due to her not being a virgin anymore. Her mother asked her on several occasions if she was pregnant. She would tell her no and reassure her by telling her she planned to go to college. She would add on that she didn't have time for babies.

About a week later, Princess couldn't take the sickness any longer. She figured she was ill with some sort of virus. Princess had tried another test while no one was home and she looked down this time and discovered it had two lines. She was pregnant.

Reality hit her and she was devastated. She cried because she thought her life was now over. Princess felt like she was unfit to be a mother. She was young and didn't really know how to care for a baby.

She had become pregnant while a member of the church and the life she lived wasn't pleasing unto God anymore. Princess didn't have anyone that could be by her side when she told the soon to be father the news. He told her that he didn't want anything to do with the child. He lied saying, he was moving out of town to San Francisco with his father. Princess pleaded with him to help. She had just graduated, what was she going to do with a baby? She didn't want to tell her mother because she was afraid of what she would say. She had to tell someone. They would eventually find out because her appearance was rapidly changing. She had to tell them the truth.

She was 3 months along when she found out she was with child. She was hurt, because she believed her life was ruined. The father wanted nothing to do with or the baby. The perfect family she longed for he didn't have her child's father around, he didn't want anything to do with her. All she wanted was a perfect family with lots of love and marriage. Later on, within the next four weeks, it was now time for Princess to get her first ultrasound and boy was that baby cute. Her mother couldn't believe that she was with child because Princess would always say, "I'm not ever having kids until I get married and graduate from college."

She really wanted to go to college, it felt like she threw a whole full scholarship down the drain because she was of the child. All she could think about was how much she had accomplished throughout her life. When she was going through hell, her motivation to continue pressing forward was one day she would be able to reach her dream. It was starting to seem like her dream was blown out the window because now it was time for her to raise a child without a job or its father.

It was the day she would learn the sex of her baby. Princess really didn't want to move when the receptionist called her, but was extremely anxious to know the baby's sex. As they went back into the room her mother was alongside her, she was happy and wanted to know the sex of her first grandchild just as bad. The doctor revealed she was pregnant with a girl. Princess really didn't want to keep the baby girl but she had to think of it as a blessing from God.

Princess was in a state of depression because she felt like she let God down and threw her future away. She didn't have her daughter's father around because he didn't want anything to do with Princess anymore, it seemed like all he wanted her for was her body and once he got what he had wanted that poor girl suffered. Now she had to raise the baby on her own. She wasn't quite fit to raise a baby girl in this world filled with killings, fighting, and crack heads and alcoholics on every corner. *Why would I get pregnant at this time,* she thought to herself. She was unworthy and didn't know how to turn to God and ask for forgiveness because she would be having a baby out of wedlock. Many people were criticizing her and she began to get overwhelmed. She experienced some low self-esteem, bitterness, anger, and was fed up, ready to take her life all over again.

Princess felt like she did a stupid thing and that God would never forgive her. All she wanted was a big happy family but her daughter's father didn't want that. He began to hurt her so many ways. He blocked access to himself on all social media sites, disrespected her, and called her names. He told her, "I only wanted the sex. It was good while it lasted." Princess was pissed and wanted to cut him. Now she'd be stuck raising a baby alone and he thought it was a game. She began to doubt God and didn't care about church anymore because now she felt unworthy and unfit to do things in God's will.

She had wanted to fill that empty space that her child's father left which was simply broken. All she needed was to find someone perfect, that would treat her and the baby with respect, and love Princess for the amazing young lady that she had become. It seemed like she couldn't find the right guy and she began to get weary because she couldn't understand why it was so hard to find somebody to love her. Princess thought God was making her suffer because she had a baby without being married and she was saved. She just couldn't understand why it seemed like her whole life was falling down by the wayside. Despite her depression, Princess had to keep on going so that her baby girl could be a light in her life where all of the dark places seemed lonely and cold.

She thought that God wouldn't use her anymore because of what she had done and how she committed sins even while on the usher board, praying, fasting, reading the word, dancing, and shouting. She was certain God was going to take her out but He had another plan for her life.

Chapter 8

Psalms 18:6 In my distress I called upon the LORD, and cried unto my God: he heard my voice out of his temple, and my cry came before him, even into his ears.

Four months later Princess went into labor. She felt as if the Lord was getting ready to open her eyes and bless her with something that would change her life. After all the hell she'd been through, now she was getting ready to push out a miracle.

Princess gave birth to a baby girl and named her, Isabella Rebecca Smith. She was delivered December 16th, 2014 at 3:30pm. It was such a blessing; she was so adorable and looked just like her mommy.

Princess was suffering from postpartum depression because she experienced some heartache and pain over her child's father not being around. Nobody was calling her to see if she was okay. Princess' baby had to stay inside the NICU after she was born because she was having complications. She wasn't able to comfort her baby and hated seeing her laying there with all those tubes on her. Princess was stressed out.

Princess was discharged home but had to leave Isabella there. She had a nervous breakdown. When Princess got home, she tried to drink water and bleach mix so she could die. She felt like she wasn't worthy to be a mommy for the pain that she had to see Isabella go through before she had left the hospital.

Later that night into the next day, Princess had started to turn red and pale she had drunk a bottle of alcohol and then took some Percocet's for her pain. Along with that Princess had smoked about 5 blunts back to back. She started to throw up blood and they had to call an ambulance for her because they didn't know what was going on. She wasn't talking very much and her skin was extremely hot. By the time they got her to the hospital they had to rush her straight into a room.

Princess' eyes rolled into the back of her head. They had tried to put an IV in so she could get fluid in her because at any moment she could pass out or suddenly die. Princess's blood pressure and pulse were very high. They had to try to get that down because she was already at risk. She began to cry and said, "I just want my baby girl's pain to be over. *Why me God! Can You just help me heal my Isabella!!!?*"

When the doctors came in Princess' eyes, were open and the doctor began to talk to her. Princess was telling her that she didn't remember what happened, all she was trying to do was save her daughter's life by taking her own. It was almost night time and Princess hadn't seen her daughter at all that day but she was about to be discharged. Once she got out of the EP Deliverance Emergency Room, she went right upstairs to go see Isabella. Isabella was inside Princess arms, she started to cry out unto the Lord because all she wanted for her child was to be healed. That very next day Princess, feeling a little better, went over to the hospital so her Aunt Hanna could pray over the baby.

Princess believed that the Lord had heard her cry because all she wanted was her baby girl home with her and sometimes she would like if she could spend more time with her. Going up to the hospital everyday was extremely upsetting to Princess. She went to EP Deliverance Hospital one last time, and while holding her baby, she realized that Isabella didn't have tubes anymore. The Lord had heard Princess' cry. God knew the plan that if she had brought Isabella out Princess's whole life would turn around. Isabella was able to come home after being in the hospital for 10 days after her delivery to this world. Her mother Princess was so delighted because she was now able to care for her beautiful baby girl.

God heard Princess cry even when she was on the verge of dying. God saw fit to wipe every tear from her eyes and speak to Princess, declaring that she shall live because there's a little blessing that needs her so she had to straighten up and open up her eyes. Princess had to keep the faith and put her trust in God so that she would know that her daughter would be healed. Princess had to get a wakeup call and promise God that if he had saved her life and touched her baby girl that she would serve him forever.

Chapter 9

Romans 6:14-19 For sin shall not have dominion over you: for ye are not under the law, but under grace. What then? Shall we sin, because we are not under the law, but under grace? God forbid. Know ye not, that to whom ye yield yourselves servants to obey, his servants ye are to whom ye obey; whether of sin unto death, or of obedience unto righteousness? But God be thanked, that ye were the servants of sin, but ye have obeyed from the heart that form of doctrine which was delivered you. Being then made free from sin, ye became the servants of righteousness. I speak after the manner of men because of the infirmity of your flesh: for as ye have yielded your members servants to uncleanness and to iniquity unto iniquity; even so now yield your members servants to righteousness unto holiness.

Princess was attending a church called Victory in God Ministries where the Apostle was Margaret. Princess was an excellent usher and loved to serve. She loved her Apostle dearly. She was like a spiritual mother and she had never given up on Princess because she knew that she was one of God's chosen. Apostle Margaret would always provoke her to trust in God and stay the course even with all the hell she went through. She assured her that no matter what she did, God would still use her for His glory.

Princess called Apostle Margaret "Nana" because she showed her the same love her grandmother did when she was living. Apostle spoke a life changing word into her life, but she would still go home and go through the same thing over and over. She would just smoke and drink to ease her pain, that was her excuse for sinning. Apostle Margaret had to let her know to wait on God and he will see her through. Assuring her "no weapon formed against her shall be able to prosper, and every tongue that rises shall be condemned." Apostle Margaret would ask her to usher at the door because she saw that there was love in Princess; her smile would embrace the people of God when they came in.

Apostle would preach a word and she would cry all of the time because the message would bless her soul. Every time she would go up for prayer, the Apostle always ministered to her and let her know that everything would be alright. She would say, "Stay the course, don't give up on God." Even if she was young and dealt with major issues, the word of God would strengthen her and see her through. God heard Princess' cries and Apostle Margaret would let her know, "Baby, weeping may endure for a night but there's joy coming in the morning. Keep the good fight of faith and stay connected to God, He will see you through every test and trial. The victory belongs to you." Needless to say Princess had all but given up on church.

Isabella was getting big, she was about to be 5 months old. It was time for Princess to start fresh so that her baby girl could be raised up the right way. Princess had to change her lifestyle and get delivered from all of the bondage that she was dealing with which caused her to act how she was acting when it came to taking her life. She intended on going back to church and giving her life to God for real; when she did, she found another church home.

She was visiting a church called Miracle Life Outreach Ministry. She really enjoyed herself every time she went and her daughter was embraced with so much love. They constantly prayed for her and always gave her words of encouragement. It was like God knew what she needed because he sent some great people in her life. They encouraged her and let her know that just because she had a baby out of wedlock doesn't mean that God looks at her any different. They would always say to her, "Do not allow having a baby to stop you from pressing towards your dreams and goals."

She had to put her faith in God and got free from all of her strongholds and allowed her flesh to die. As a young mother it was hard to realize that in God everything will be alright even though she grew up in church, all people make mistakes. All the hell she went through drove her life into a dark place and she had to search for God in order for her life to be free and built back up again. She had to realize that the only thing that would keep her was to surrender herself fully to God and trust in him.

Deliverance was a bit hard. She was still drinking and smoking weed every day after church. Until one day, she had her baby and was super high to the point she almost dropped poor Isabella. That night she had to make a choice, whether she was going to live for God or serve man. A small voice came upon her and laughed but she couldn't recognize it. Then another voice came and said, "Daughter just give it up, you can't fit in with the world anymore, you are made different." She was struggling and didn't know how to get out but she began to look into her daughter's eyes and cry because she felt like she was setting a bad example and knew her daughter was a blessing from God. Princess would start going to church and pray at night trying to get closer to God. So that very next week she went to church and gave her life back to Christ.

She joined the church Miracle Life Outreach Ministries because it was something special about that church and Princess was happy there. She had felt the presence of God like nowhere else. She felt like God sent some great people in her life that would never give up on her and let her know that in Him she still can make it along the way. She had to search for God in order for her life to be free and built back up again.

When she started attending the new church it was like she found God even the more. She sold out to God wholeheartedly. God had sent people into her life that would give her love and surround her with lots of wisdom. Her desire was that God would fill her up with the word that will sustain her and set her free from all of her troubles.

The church she attended had inspiring leaders, Pastor Kenneth and Grace Brown. She felt like she was in the right place because they would feed her with the word and when she didn't understand it she could ask her leaders for help. Those were the kind of leaders she had needed in her life at that moment. There were also young people who would look up to her but she couldn't understand why.

Pastor Grace didn't really care about the amount of official members, she had a passion for God's people and their hearts. Princess walked into the church on Sunday and she felt something different, it was like a wave of Glory. Pastors Grace and Kenneth were truly anointed. They would always lift her up, so that she would understand that the pain hurts but God will get all of the glory if she just seek his face and stay in his will. Pastor Grace helped her along her journey so that she could be a successful mother and someone great in God. They pushed her all the way and it really amazed her when she came to the church, how they showed her the love of a mother and father that she had never gotten from her own parents. They would treat her as if she was their blood child because they could see that she was hurting inside and could relate to what she was going through from time to time.

Sometimes she would disobey God, but Pastor Grace had to explain to her that obedience is better than sacrifice; she had to have faith the size of a mustard seed and not give up on God. Her pastor had seen something great in her and knew that the enemy was trying to stop her from getting to the place where God wanted her to be. Pastor Kenneth gave her the understanding that even though she's hurting because of her baby's father, that the only significant other she needed in her life right now was God. He would help her through all of her trials and tribulations and she will come out victorious and God would one day give her a man that would add greatness and success to her and her daughter's life. Her pastors truly lived what they preach and became Princess' biggest inspiration because they live for God for real.

Within a month or so her church was putting on a youth conference and her pastor had put her on the program to read a scripture. This was going to be Princess first time reading a scripture so she was a nervous wreck. She didn't know what scripture to read she went to God and He gave her Romans 8:28 "And we know that all things work together for good to them that love God, to them who are called according to His purpose." Before she began to read, her Pastor told her to read it with power. She started to read and all the nervousness left her body. The word was so powerful and she knew that God was leading her the right way because it tied into the word that her Pastor was preaching.

Princess would constantly say that her Pastor blesses her spirit every time she sees her or hear her preach the word she knew that there was a reason why God had her come to this ministry. Pastor Grace had such an anointing on her life that will truly be a blessing to so many people because she was kind and sweet. God changed Princess' whole life when he sent this wonderful couple into her life. They showed her the power and love of God in a dark place. They believed in Princess and wanted to get her to place she needed to be free and delivered from everything she dealt with growing up until now with her beautiful baby girl Isabella.

She had to believe in herself as well as her church did because she was called by God and has a great anointing on her life. She loved to pray and help young people and believed that if God did it for her that he would do it for other young mothers and young adults that were going through the same stuff she went through. She wanted to break the curse in her generation. She had started to receive prophecies from her Pastors. They tell her, "Princess, God is going to do wonderful things in your life just watch. Stay in alignment with him.

He got your back. If he did it for me and my house then he's going to do it for you as well."

Pastor Grace started to ask Princess some questions like, "Do you believe God will deliver you from all of your troubles? Do you think God will make a way of escape for you?" Pastor Kenneth would say, "Look at me. Where would I be without God, I should've been dead and gone a long time ago but God say fit to set me free." They constantly provoked Princess to go after God on a personally level and get to know who He is to her personally. They always had deep conversation with Princess to keep her on the right track...winning! Princess often explained to Pastor Grace that the enemy continued to attack her. He was stopping her from moving forward. Pastor Grace would often encourage and empowering her with words like, "Listen daughter God is with you! Fight the enemy off in the spirit and he will flee. Use your gift of the Holy Spirit and defeat the devil! You are powerful! Stand! Keep pushing beyond what you see and how you feel! You shall live and not die! Keep praying until the mountain moves out of your life!"

Princess was crying out to God as she was inside her Pastor's office because she was fighting against depression. She didn't want to be depressed. God had done some great things in her life thus far. The devil kept reminding her of her past from her childhood. The devil kept telling her that Isabella would go through the same thing. Princess knew she needed help and needed it fast because her mind was all over the place. Her Pastor grabbed her tight and said, "Listen daughter no matter what, I got you. God would take you through the process of getting healed in your mind and heart. You and your daughter will be victorious. You will be greater than your past!" Princess started learning of God as her personal way maker, healer, strength and mind regulator. She learned how to defeat the devil with praise, prayer, worship and the Word.

That next day she was ready to defeat the enemy early in the morning she prayed unto God and decreed and declared her day. She was anointed for this and the enemy was throwing distractions but she continued to press through the crowd like the women with the issue of blood so she could get her deliverance. Every day she renewed her mind and knew that God was protecting her with surrounding angels and covering her and her baby girl with the blood of Jesus. She had to get her mind right or the mental illness would kill her and have her stay stuck in a place where she would be depressed, stressed, and just wanting to die. She wanted to be free and break every curse that was put on her so that she could spiritually birth out something new in her bloodline. She was gonna break the generational curse off her life. She believed that she was who

God said she was and that she was going to walk into the authority that God gave her and continue to do what He called her to do because there was greatness inside of Princess. She wanted to walk in the same confidence she seen in her grandmothers face when she tried to commit suicide the first time. Her grandmother was at peace because she knew God was in control. As Princess was getting her deliverance God was using her with intercessory prayer in the church, and exalting the youth Sunday services not knowing that it was all working out for her good. She had to make up in her mind that she wanted to be totally done with doing things of the world and just live for God 100%.

He sent great people in her life that were her biggest supporters. They help her grown in God and also taught her more about the word which let her know she was chosen, a royal priesthood that God needed in the kingdom. She had to understand that there was greatness inside of her and know that she was who God says she is no matter what she hears or what people say about her. It was now time for her to get over people and the things she dealt with throughout life so that she could get fully delivered. She was learning has the power to speak and God will turn it around for her good.

She continued on going to church and her Pastor would constantly remind her that she was special to God and that he will work a miracle out in her favor all she had to do was believe and trust in his promises. Pastor Grace had began to talk to her about personal things she was dealing with and all she could do was cry. Pastor Grace would remind her that mighty are the works of His hands and His name is above all names there's nobody greater than Him. She was always encouraging Princess.

Being at this church God allowed people to believe in her even the more and they spoke life into her. She was finally at a point that giving up was no longer an option for her to choose. Other's need her to show them how she made it out. She had to know that God would never leave her nor forsake her. She had to be strong for her baby girl and family

All the praying and crying at night it wasn't in vain because God was allowing people to let her know that her breakthrough was coming and that he still had his hand on her. She just had to keep walking in the promises of God.

Chapter 10

Romans 3:24 God did it for us. Out of sheer generosity he put us in right standing with himself. A pure gift. He got us out of the mess we're in and restored us to where he always wanted us to be. And he did it by means of Jesus Christ.

After having Isabella, Princess went without a job for several months, living from welfare check to welfare check each month. She wanted to move out and get her own place for her and her daughter. She couldn't understand why God wasn't making a way and answering her prayers. Every night she cried herself to sleep because she couldn't take living life the way she was. She was delivered enough to remain faithful to God and was ready to receive his promises. She didn't know that it all was part of a process, and while she was going through the process, God was lining something up for her and Isabella.

One of Princess' former teachers; Mrs. Epic contacted her and told her, her place of employment was hiring for a temporary position. She instructed her to send her resume in so she could give it to her boss. She did. She had to remind herself that if God did it before then he can do it again. Princess started to thank God in advance for the blessing and gave him praise. The next day they called her to schedule an interview and she was extremely excited and nervous.

Princess went home that night and prayed that God would bless her with this job. She was fresh out of nursing school and ready for a fresh start. She walked into the interview and couldn't wait until she left. She was eager to see how she had done. Mrs. Epic called her to let her know she had gotten the job. After all the hell that she went through, she couldn't believe that God did it for her.

God was starting to open doors in her life because He understood the desires of her heart. She started at her new job June of 2016, Princess was so successful at her work that her employers kept putting off ending the temporary position. She was excellent at what she did and they needed her in order to get the job done.

Princess continued praying and remained steadfast in her faith. Later on, just before the year was out, God showed her favor and she was blessed with a two bedroom apartment. Princess didn't have enough money to cover the move-in cost, but God sent her help. All she had to do was trust in him and seek his face and everything she needed was worked out in faith. She moved in and decorated her house with her Pastor. God was beginning to blow her mind because now this temporary job became permanent. People thought she wasn't going to be successful at living on her own but she maintained well.

It's definitely a blessing that God opened up doors for Princess and she gave him praise every day. She now has a youth prayer line, ushers at her church faithfully, is assistant to her leader, works with the young people at her church, ministers from time to time, and, most of all, loves God with all of her heart.

With all the hell she went through, God saw fit to reach out and save her. He chose someone like her to be something great and He has continued to bless. GOD DID IT!!!!!!

God will allow us to go through and allow us to see we have the ability and power to overcome. God continues to stick by us, all we have to do is continue to be pure in Him and understand that He makes the impossible possible. We have to recognize that he will forever be in the midst of any storm with us. Even though we tend to fall, God is there to lift us right back up. Trust in Him, you are more than a conqueror. Don't give up on God. He will see you through. Remember God Can and Will Do It!!!!!!

"CiCi Smallz Thoughts"

Though Princess went through a lot of struggle and pain, God brought her all the way out! Some of her pain was due to the hands of others. Some of her pain was due to her own decisions. Regardless of the pain and where it came from, God healed her! She walked around for years wearing a mask. A mask made up of false realities! Underneath the mask was so much pain that was killing Princess from the inside out. No one's situation is hopeless! It doesn't matter how much pain or how long it's been there. Though it may be difficult to see any way out of the pain you're in, God is truly <u>able</u> and <u>willing</u> to set you free. He will give you His peace that surpasses all understanding and it will keep your heart and mind! It won't be an easy task but THROUGH CHRIST JESUS, YOU CAN DO ALL THINGS! HE STRENGTHENS US! Your healing process starts with you allowing Jesus to come into your heart! You do that by asking Him to forgive you of all your sins, confessing with your mouth that He is Lord and believing He died on the cross for you! (Romans 10:9) After you've done that, He considers you His child! JESUS IS YOUR LORD and SAVIOR! Now you must start by letting go and letting God! This will also be a process...you have to learn of who He is and who you are to Him! Don't go through in silence. Reach out to someone that can help you! Get connected to people that will encourage, empower & help you through your process, as well as get connected to a bible teaching, God (only) exalting church and start walking in your FREEDOM!

Your story may not be identical to Princess' but I'm sure you will find yourself in there somewhere. I DID & BECAUSE OF JESUS, I'M LIVING IN FREEDOM! –CiCi Smallz

www.ingramcontent.com/pod-product-compliance
Lightning Source LLC
Chambersburg PA
CBHW030339020726
47493CB00004B/1338